TEEN TITANS GO!

ROBIN RULES!

Adapted by **Annie Auerbach**

Based on the episodes
"Driver's Ed" written by **Tab Murphy**
and
"Super Robin" written by **Adam Stein**

LITTLE, BROWN AND COMPANY
New York   Boston

Little, Brown and Company

Hachette Book Group
1290 Avenue of the Americas, New York, NY 10104
Visit us at lb-kids.com

Little, Brown and Company is a division of Hachette Book Group, Inc.
The Little, Brown name and logo are trademarks of Hachette Book Group, Inc.

The publisher is not responsible for websites (or their content)
that are not owned by the publisher.

First Edition: October 2014

Library of Congress Cataloging-in-Publication Data

Auerbach, Annie.
  Robin rules! / adapted by Annie Auerbach. — First edition.
     pages cm. — (Teen Titans go!)
  ISBN 978-0-316-33333-7 (trade pbk.) — ISBN 978-0-316-33334-4 (ebook)
  — ISBN 978-0-316-33335-1 (library edition ebook)
  I. Title.
PZ7.A9118Rob 2014
[E]—dc23
                                                             2014007624

10 9 8 7 6 5 4 3 2 1

RRD-C

Printed in the United States of America

CONTENTS

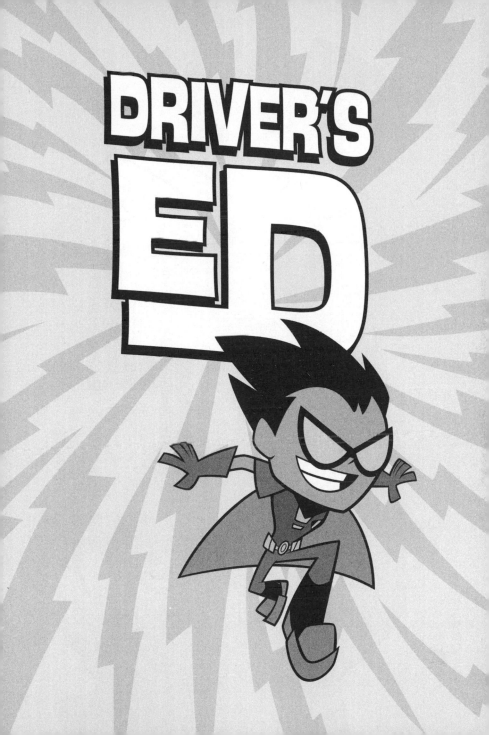

CHAPTER 1

One Monday afternoon, Beast Boy was sitting in his bedroom playing a video game. Not only was he doing well, his victory looked assured. His eyes glistened with tears of joy.

"This is going to be the greatest achievement of my life," he said, practically weeping.

Just then, Robin kicked open the bedroom

door. "Beast Boy! Emergency! No time to explain. Come on, get the car! Gotta go!"

In an instant, Beast Boy flung down the controller and followed Robin out of the room. Beast Boy had been so close to winning the game, and now…it was game over.

Robin sat in the passenger seat next to Beast Boy as the Teen Titans' car raced down the street.

"What's the emergency?" asked Beast Boy.

Robin's eyes narrowed. "Got a monster to deal with."

But Beast Boy was in for a surprise. Robin ordered him to turn into the Burger Splode drive-thru.

"A monster case of the munchies!" explained Robin. He leaned across Beast Boy and shouted into the drive-thru intercom. "A cheeseburger, fries, milk shake, and a small side salad. Stat!"

Beast Boy sat fuming behind the wheel. He gave up his video game win for this?!

On Tuesday, Cyborg hooked himself up for his weekly data backup. A USB cable ran from the computer and plugged right into his head. A large warning displayed on the screen: **CAUTION! DO NOT REMOVE CABLE DURING BACKUP. SOME DATA MAY BE LOST.**

"Man, these backups seem like they take longer every week," said a bored Cyborg.

At that moment, Robin kicked open the door.

"Cyborg! Emergency! No time to explain!" said Robin. "Come on, get the car. We gotta go!" He grabbed Cyborg, pulling him from the cable.

The screen flashed: **WARNING! DATA LOST!**

But Cyborg wasn't there to see it. He was already in the driver's seat of the car, zooming along. When Robin told him to pull over at the Game Bear store, Cyborg was confused.

Robin jumped out of the car before Cyborg

could say a word. In a flash, Robin was in and out of the store. He held up a new video game.

"Check it out," Robin said smugly. "Dog Simulator 2000!"

Cyborg was so shocked and annoyed, he swatted the game out of Robin's hands and onto the ground.

On Wednesday, Starfire stood in the living room and removed yellow berries from an alien plant, placing them into a bowl. Her pet—a small, pink mutant moth larva named Silkie—lay next to the plant and tried to eat the berries.

"You cannot eat the berries, Silkie," said Starfire. "They are bad for you."

Just then, Robin crashed through the window and landed on the table.

"Starfire! Emergency!" said Robin. "No time to explain. Come on, get the car. We gotta go!"

As Robin and Starfire ran off together, Silkie saw his chance. He crawled over to the berries and ate the entire bowl. Instantly, his face swelled up and became puffy. Uh-oh.

Meanwhile, Starfire raced off in the car, with Robin next to her. When Robin asked to be dropped off at a D.J. Aqualad concert, all he said was, "Pick me up in an hour. Thank you!"

Starfire's eyes glowed green with anger.

On Thursday, Raven was in her room.

A demon roared and tried to come through a portal on her wall. Raven fired a bolt of magic at the demon, trying to banish it. "Back, foul demon!" As she was about to cast a final spell to send him permanently back into the portal, Robin tore a hole in the ceiling and dropped down.

"Raven! Emergency!" yelled Robin. "No time to explain. Come on, get the car. We gotta go!" He grabbed her and zipped out.

The demon hesitantly opened an eye and looked around. Surprised that it had been left alone, it smiled evilly and flew off, looking for trouble.

In the car, Raven and Robin sped off. With Robin's directions, they ended up at the beach.

"Woo-hoo!" yelled Robin as he grabbed his surfboard and hit the waves.

Raven's anger hit a boiling point. She had stopped battling a dangerous demon to give Robin a ride to the beach?!

CHAPTER 2

On Friday, Raven, Cyborg, Beast Boy, and Starfire were hanging out in the living room at Titans Tower. They weren't surprised when Robin burst in yelling, "Guys! Emergency! No time to explain. Come on, get the car. We gotta go!" He ran out.

But no one followed him.

So Robin ran back in and screamed,

"Guys! Emergency! Car! Go! Now!" He ran out again. Still, none of the other Titans moved.

After a moment, Robin walked back in and said sheepishly, "Uh…guys? Emergency?"

Raven was immediately skeptical. "Oh, yeah?" she said. "What's the big emergency, Robin?"

He held up a flyer. "Everything's half off at the dollar store," he explained excitedly.

Cyborg couldn't believe what he was hearing. "Man, all week you've been bumming rides for stupid stuff. You know you messed up my weekly backup, right? You're lucky I didn't lose any important data!"

Next to him on the couch was Starfire's pet, Silkie, who was still all puffed up from eating the berries. "I must agree with Cyborg," said Starfire. "It is most irritating."

"Thank you," Cyborg told her. Then he realized he didn't know who he was thanking! His laser eye automatically scanned Starfire, but he still couldn't identify her. He nudged Beast Boy with his elbow. "Who's that orange girl?"

Apparently, Cyborg *was* missing some

15

important data! Malfunction sparks whizzed around his head.

"Why can't you just drive yourself, dude?" Beast Boy asked Robin.

"Uh…" began Robin. He cleared his throat. "My license was suspended."

"What?!" exclaimed Beast Boy.

"Yeah," Robin said, uncomfortably. "I was in a little fender bender."

(Actually, Robin *totally* wrecked the Batmobile!)

"Anyway," continued Robin, trying to get back on track, "I found a guy on the Internet. He says he'll help me get my license back, no problemo."

Raven wasn't so sure. "Sounds kind of sketchy, Robin."

"Nah," replied Robin. "It's on the level. Besides, how can I not pass? I'm a *master driver!*"

CHAPTER 3

The next day, Robin went to the location where he was supposed to meet the guy, a driver's education teacher. He looked around, but didn't see anyone. Then he noticed a beat-up car with a sign reading STUDENT on the top of it. When Robin walked up to the car, he saw a note attached to the window. The note read: **Get in. Start engine.**

So Robin did. He put on his seat belt, started the car, and turned on the radio, trying to find a decent station. When he did, he turned it up full blast and began rocking out to the music.

Robin had no idea that his music was covering up a very important sound: that of a blaring bank alarm! Half a block away, a robber ran out of the bank holding a blue duffel bag crammed with money. He ran up to the car that Robin was in and opened the hatchback. He put the money in the back of the car and pulled out a clipboard. Then he sat in the car's passenger seat, put on his seat belt, and turned off the radio.

"My name is Ed," he told Robin. His voice was a monotone and not what you'd expect from a bank robber! "I'll be your driving instructor."

Robin laughed. "Ed? As in 'driver's ed'?"

Ed was *not* amused. "Just Ed." Then he got down to business. "The way this works is that every time you fail to comply with an instruction, I make a deduction. Too many deductions, you fail."

Just then, Robin finally noticed the bank alarm. "Hey, what's that noise? Is that—?"

Ed ignored him and said, "Pull out into traffic and proceed through the intersection."

"But what about the—?" Robin began.

Ed marked the sheet on his clipboard. "Aaaaand that's a deduction."

"Okay, right, right," said Robin, trying to focus on getting his license back. He pulled away from the curb. "I'm going."

20

A bank guard raced out of the bank and began shooting at the car.

Robin cocked his head. "I swear that sounds like—"

"Eyes front," Ed instructed.

Robin nodded nervously. "Sorry."

"That's a deduction," said Ed, making another check mark on his list. "Left here."

Robin turned left, but since he didn't use his turn signal, he received yet another deduction.

"Aw, man," said Robin. This was not going well.

Suddenly, half a dozen police cars appeared, their sirens blaring. They were catching up to Robin's car.

"Increase your speed," Ed said calmly to Robin.

"If you say so," said Robin. He stomped on the gas.

"Now turn right," Ed said.

Robin wrenched the wheel to the right. The cops behind them did the same thing.

"Are you sure—?" Robin started to say.

"Deduction," replied Ed. "Now go left."

Robin turned and sped over a fire hydrant. Water shot up into the air like a fountain.

"Deduction," Ed said again. "Hard right."

"But there's nowhere to turn right," said Robin. On the right was the ocean!

Ed didn't seem to care. The police cars were still on their tail. "TWO deductions," he said. "Hard right!"

Robin did as he was told, and the car smashed through a guardrail and flew off the cliff. It soared through the air and landed in the bay.

As the car slowly sank into the water, Ed said, "I think we're finished here."

"So...how did I do?" Robin asked hesitantly.

Ed finished writing on his pad and tore off the top sheet, handing it to Robin. It had one word on it: **FAIL**.

CHAPTER 4

Robin stood in front of the refrigerator at Titans Tower. He was staring at all the red marks on his test.

"So, you failed your driver's test?" said Raven.

All the other Teen Titans laughed.

"*Master driver*, huh?" Cyborg guffawed.

Starfire giggled. "Laughing at your short-

comings makes us all feel better about our-
selves." Then she flew over to Robin and
tried to act nicer. "It is okay," she told him.
"A lot of people fail the test of driving."

From the table, Cyborg looked at Starfire
curiously. "Will someone please tell me
who that strange woman is?" He still didn't
recognize her.

"Look, I'm a great driver," Robin insisted to Starfire. "I'm just not a great test taker. The good thing is, I can keep retaking the test until I pass. And I *will* pass! Because I am a *master driver*!"

As soon as Robin left the room, Raven looked at the others. "He's going to fail, isn't he?"

Cyborg nodded. "Big-time."

Later that week, outside a pawnshop, Robin met up with Ed again. As before, Ed stole lots of cash and used Robin as the driver of the getaway vehicle. Once again, Robin had the radio blaring and couldn't hear the shop's alarm going off.

As Robin drove away, he turned to Ed and

28

said, "So last time, I think you freaked me out a little, but now I'm ready."

At that moment, shots from a police officer's gun nearly hit the car.

"Did you hear that?" Robin exclaimed. "It sounds like—"

Ed immediately looked down at his clipboard. "That's going to be—"

"Okay, okay!" Robin said quickly. "No deductions!" He sped off, with a slew of police cars in pursuit.

"This music is terrible," Ed said, wrinkling his nose. "That's a deduction."

Robin became flooded with determination. He was *not* going to fail again. He pressed the gas pedal to the floor and zoomed right over the roadblock that had been set up by the Jump City Police

Department. The car flew through the air—and landed safely on the ground. But that wasn't good enough for Ed.

"Only three seconds in the air?" said Ed, looking at a stopwatch. "Deduction!"

Ed instructed Robin to drive straight into Food Bear, a local supermarket. A line of police cars followed them inside. As Robin drove, Ed rolled down his window and picked up some bananas and crackers along the way.

"I asked you to turn down the cereal aisle," Ed said, annoyed.

Robin sighed. "I know...that's a deduction."

It was the ultimate game of cat and mouse between Robin and the police cars. Up and down the aisles they sped, but in the end, the police cars just crashed into one another. Robin and Ed zoomed out of the market scot-free.

Outside, Ed finished marking up Robin's latest test results. He wrote a big **FAIL** on it—again!

"Meet me for a retake in front of the casino," said Ed.

Robin put his head in his hands. He wondered if he would *ever* pass his driving test.

CHAPTER 5

The following day, Robin had the car waiting outside the casino, just as Ed had instructed. As before, Ed stashed some cash in the back and then had Robin drive off. Along the way, it was one fake deduction after another, and Robin failed again.

For the next several days, Ed had Robin meet him at places like the Money Factory

and even the end of the rainbow—where they encountered a very angry leprechaun. Ed would steal and Robin would drive, over and over again.

Meanwhile, in another part of the city, the demon that had escaped from Raven poked its head up from a manhole, wearing the cover like a hat. When it saw the Teen Titans sitting outside at a local coffee shop, the demon fled, not wanting to get caught.

At the table, Cyborg extended his telescopic eye right at Starfire, whom he still didn't recognize.

"How about you just tell me who you are?" Cyborg said to her. "We went to school together, right? You look a lot like my cousin. Did we eat at the same restaurant the other night?"

Starfire didn't know what to say.

Raven just rolled her eyes. Then, suddenly, she spotted someone familiar across the street in front of a jewelry store.

"Hey, is that Robin?" asked Raven.

The others looked over. It was indeed Robin, sitting behind the wheel of a car.

"Huh," said Beast Boy. "He's supposed to be meeting his driver's ed instructor. I don't know why he's in front of a jewelry store."

Wee-o! Wee-o! Wee-o!

The alarm at the Diamonds Aplenty jewelry store rang out. The Teen Titans watched as a man carrying a stash of stolen cash and diamonds jumped into the car's passenger seat.

"Looks like it's because *Robin's* the getaway driver," said Raven.

Starfire's eyes became wide. "Surely Robin is not aware he is aiding and abetting a criminal."

Cyborg stood up. "Well, that's why we've got to warn him!"

CHAPTER 6

The Teen Titans headed to their car, and Cyborg sat in the driver's seat. They had to stop Robin before it was too late. Cyborg floored it and was tailgating Robin in no time. He honked the horn and the other Titans waved and yelled, trying to get Robin's attention.

Robin looked behind him, surprised at

what he saw. "What are they doing here?" he wondered. "Oh…to laugh at me." He imagined them saying, "No superpowers *and* can't drive." Robin steeled his jaw. "I'll show them!" he vowed.

"Make a right here," Ed said from the passenger seat.

"Stow it, Ed!" exclaimed Robin. "I've got this one!" Pumping the gas, he cranked the wheel and burned rubber.

Behind him, Cyborg downshifted and turned on the rear blasters, giving his car super-speed.

Robin zoomed all around the city. He raced toward a building—and then actually drove up the side of it! Cyborg, however, crashed right into the building. After backing up, Cyborg was able to drive up the building's

side and continue to give chase to Robin. Both cars sped and jumped from building roof to building roof.

Robin loved the chase. Ed…well, he felt a little nauseous.

With some quick moves, Robin launched the car into space, easily navigating around some asteroids in his way. The same couldn't be said for Cyborg, who managed to follow Robin into space, but hit those asteroids like his car was a ball in a pinball machine. **Crash! Slam! Bam!**

As the two cars plunged back toward Earth, the only one enjoying the ride was Robin. Both Ed and the Teen Titans were scared and nervous. Bouncing off a rainbow, Robin made it safely back to the ground and screeched to a halt. Close by, Cyborg and the other Titans landed, but their car exploded on impact.

"Nice driving, Cyborg," Raven said sarcastically.

Just then, one of the tires from the Titans' car fell from the sky and conked Cyborg on the head. It rattled the data in his skull.

"Hey, when did Starfire get here?" he asked, finally recognizing her. The bump on the head had done the trick.

Nearby, Ed staggered out of the car, panting. He thought that was the scariest and worst ride of his life. He gulped as he approached Robin. "You pass," said Ed, tearing off the paper and handing it to Robin.

"YES!" cheered Robin.

Ed clenched his fists. "But only because I never want you as a getaway driver again!" he screamed. Then he smirked and said, "I was using you the whole time, and you couldn't see it."

"Nope, I knew," Robin said confidently.

Ed was shocked to hear that.

Robin put his hands on his hips. "That's why I'm not warning you about the demon."

Sure enough, the demon that had escaped earlier from Raven's room was back—and it liked the taste of driver's ed instructors. Despite Ed's screams, the demon dragged him away and through a mystic portal.

Robin walked over to the portal, proud of himself for finally passing his driving test. Robin was indeed a master—and crazy—driver!

CHAPTER 1

Wee-o! Wee-o! **The burglar alarm at the** Jump City Bank sounded as the members of the H.I.V.E. Five worked together to rob the bank of all its cash.

Billy Numerous had the ability to clone himself—which was great for creating a human chain to pass heavy money bags to the getaway truck. Gizmo used his technological genius to build a flying contraption. With it, he was able to transfer loads of gold coins to the truck.

From the driver's seat, See-More used his eye helmet to spot trouble. Namely: the arrival of the Teen Titans. He banged on the side of the truck to let the others know.

Up on top of the truck was Jinx, her magenta hair shaped like two horns. She looked into the distance and sneered, "Titans." She didn't want them messing up the bank heist, so she gathered energy into a ball and flung it at her enemies. It sent out a shock wave right toward the Teen Titans' car. **Boom!** The ball hit its target, and the passengers went flying out of the vehicle. They were safe, but the car...not so much.

It blew up into a spectacular fire. But the Teen Titans didn't care about that.

"Time to teach H.I.V.E. how to play nice," Robin said. The Teen Titans got in position.

Robin and his friends stood across from all the members of H.I.V.E., each side ready to attack. Robin motioned at the largest enemy—a villain of superhuman strength

called Mammoth. Robin then said to the others, "Since Mammoth is the biggest and baddest, he's all mine! TITANS, GO!"

Both groups charged forward, and the one-on-one battles began. Robin pointed his staff toward Mammoth and unleashed an impressive onslaught of punches and jabs on the giant. "Hi-yah! Yah! Yah!"

Starfire flew over to Billy Numerous, who split into several copies of himself. But that was no problem for Starfire. She easily blasted every single one of them with her laser-beam eyes. Since that only took a few seconds, she turned to Robin.

"May I assist you with an eye blast?" she asked.

"No way, Star," replied Robin as he continued to fight. "Mammoth's all mine." He smacked Mammoth on the head over and over.

Nearby, Beast Boy faced off against Jinx.
Before the villain could do anything, Beast
Boy turned into a T. rex. With one big
CHOMP, he captured Jinx in his mouth as if
it were a cage. With Jinx still in his mouth,
Beast Boy called to Robin. "Sure you don't
need a hand, bro? I've got two very small
ones to lend." He wiggled his ridiculously
tiny T. rex hands in the air.

Mammoth was finally slowing down a bit. The only trouble was that Robin was starting to slow down, too. "I want to make this last," Robin said, breathing heavily. "You know, to teach him a lesson."

Meanwhile, See-More spotted Raven. He tried to blast her, but she reflected it back at him, smashing the criminal into a brick wall. Cyborg flew into the air to face off against Gizmo. The small but smart crook brought out every weapon he had, but he

was no match for Cyborg. The Teen Titan turned his arm into a cannon and blasted Gizmo, sending him crashing into a parked car on the street.

Having taken care of their respective opponents, Raven, Beast Boy, and Starfire sat on the sidewalk and enjoyed a post-battle snack.

Cyborg slowly descended and landed next to the others. "Let me guess, we're waiting on Robin again," he said with a sigh.

The others nodded, and they all turned to see Robin *still* fighting Mammoth. Cyborg sat on the curb with the others and enjoyed a hot dog while he watched Robin exhaust himself.

Finally, Robin shot out a grappling hook, which wrapped around Mammoth's legs, and pulled him down. Victory!

"Yes!" shouted Robin. Then he promptly fell over from exhaustion.

"So who's carrying him home this time?" Cyborg asked.

CHAPTER 2

Back at Titans Tower, Raven, Starfire, Cyborg, and Beast Boy strolled into the living room. A few seconds later, Robin entered, dragging himself across the floor.

"Great job, Titans," Robin said, gasping for breath. "I bet you're all as exhausted as I am."

Raven shrugged. "Uh...not particularly."

"All I really did was stare in the enemy's general direction," said Starfire. She demonstrated the power of the starblasts from her eyes by zapping a plant into nothing.

Robin struggled to pull himself up onto the couch. "Love the attitude," he said. "But I know your every muscle is screaming in excruciating pain." (Robin's muscles certainly were!)

"Nope," replied Cyborg. "Don't have muscles."

Beast Boy lay comfortably on the other end of the couch. "And mine are all like, 'It's all good, dude. Peace and love.'"

Robin couldn't believe what he was hearing. None of the other Teen Titans were in pain, or exhausted, or feeling anything even close to what he was. "So, basically, thanks

to your superpowers, taking down one of the deadliest threats to the planet is 'no big deal'?"

"Uh-huh," said Beast Boy.

"Yup," agreed Raven.

"Pretty much," said Cyborg, looking up from the book he was reading.

"Exactly," Starfire added, popping her head out from the kitchen.

Robin put his hands behind his head and lay back on the couch, trying to act casual. "That's cool."

A second later, Robin let loose a scream. "AAAAAAHHH!!!" He beat his arms in frustration.

Raven looked at him. "Problem, Robin?"

"It's not fair!" shouted Robin. "I do just as much as all of you, but because you have superpowers, you get to be lazy!"

Cyborg made a face. "Lazy? You're crazy." Then, without thinking, Cyborg detached one of his arms and put it in his other hand. He then extended that arm to reach a glass

59

of juice sitting on a side table. Robin gave him a look that said, "Really?! You're not lazy?"

Cyborg looked sheepish. "It was so far away," he said, taking a sip of the juice.

Raven looked up from where she was sitting on the floor. "Sure, Robin, powers make some things easier. But mostly, they're a curse."

Robin folded his arms. "Curse? Puh-lease."

"Well, look at me," Raven offered. "Who

wants to be your friend when you're basically the spawn of an intergalactic demon?"

Beast Boy turned himself into a mole rat and went up to Robin. "She's right," said Beast Boy. "All my life, everyone has always looked at me like I'm a freak."

Cyborg pointed to his metallic knee, with a tear in his eye. "And it's been so long since I've felt the sweet sensation of knee skin," he said sadly.

Starfire floated out from the kitchen and declared, "I am going to make the meatloaf for dinner."

The Titans had no response to that announcement. So Robin got back to the problem at hand and said miserably, "The only curse would be how bad I'd make you look if I had powers."

Beast Boy shrugged his little mole rat shoulders. "Guess we'll never know, since the only way guys like you get superpowers is through horrible freak accidents."

Robin suddenly smiled, an idea forming in his head. "Horrible freak accidents... that's it!"

CHAPTER 3

In his room, Robin went to work on coming up with a way to get powers. He was tired of being the only Teen Titan without them. He set up two giant clear cylinders, which were connected by different cords and wires. He picked up a cage with a bird inside (a robin, of course) and looked at it.

"All right. Ready, buddy?" he said to the

bird. "Just going to merge our DNA. No big deal." He opened the cage and carefully grabbed the critter, who chirped in reply.

"What are the superpowers of a robin?" Robin said aloud. "Well...uh...good question. Uh...flight! Picking things up off the ground with your mouth. Crazy old bird feet. Stuff like that."

Robin put the bird into one of the large cylinders. He could barely contain his excitement. "Nothing like a little lab disaster to give you superpowers," Robin said.

He shut the cylinder's door on the animal, then went to the control panel and pushed a series of buttons. To close, he took out a giant wrench and smashed the control panel with it! *Crash!*

He raced to the other cylinder and quickly got inside.

Zap! Bang!

"Bad idea! Bad idea! Bad idea!" cried Robin. He felt like his brain and his body were frying like bacon.

After his DNA restructured and the lightning bolts stopped whizzing around him, the

smoke cleared and Robin stepped out from the cylinder. And…

Nothing had changed! Robin's plan had failed.

Or had it?

Just then, the other cylinder's door opened and the bird sprang out and did an impressive somersault. Then it pulled out a Batarang launcher, fired a grappling hook, and made its escape.

Robin suddenly grabbed his stomach and doubled over in pain. His face filled with confusion as he felt feathers spring from his ears! His feet turned into bird's feet. His mouth became a beak! Robin had turned into a sort of mutant robin!

CHAPTER 4

In the living room at Titans Tower, Cyborg was complaining.

"I can't believe my luck," he began, taking another bite of his sandwich. "I just washed my car, and it's already covered in bird droppings!"

"Sorry," said a voice from the doorway. "My bad."

The Teen Titans turned to see the mutated
Robin standing there.

Cyborg was so surprised to see this new,
birdlike Robin that he dropped his sandwich. Robin picked it up with his beak
and handed it back to Cyborg. For some

reason, Cyborg didn't really feel hungry anymore.

"What happened to you?" Raven asked Robin.

"And what are you doing pooping on my car?" added Cyborg.

"I tried to give myself superpowers," Robin explained.

"By turning yourself into a chicken?" asked Starfire.

Robin sighed. "Guess it didn't really work out like I was hoping," he said, disappointed.

Beast Boy piped up. "Does this mean you finally realize superpowers are a curse?"

"No way!" exclaimed Robin. "This doesn't count. Wait…one sec…" He popped out an egg. A crack, a scramble, and ta-da! Breakfast was served!

Robin then turned serious. "This doesn't count since I didn't get any powers," he said.

Raven shook her head. "I almost want to give you superpowers *just* to teach you a lesson," she told him.

Robin was surprised. "You can give me powers?!" he said excitedly.

"Of course I can," said Raven. "But this would have to be something you *really* want."

SQUAWK!

Robin cleared his throat, a bit embarrassed about the noise he just made. "That was a 'yes,'" he clarified.

"Okay," Raven agreed. "But before I can, there's something you need to do."

"What?" asked Robin.

Raven rolled her eyes. "Don't play dumb. You know exactly what."

Robin clenched his beak. "I'm not doing the chicken dance for you."

"Chicken dance!" exclaimed Cyborg.

"No!" said Robin.

"Chicken dance!" Beast Boy said.

"Nope," Robin refused.

"Dance of the chicken! Dance of the chicken!" cheered Starfire.

Robin looked at the others. He realized that if he wanted to get superpowers, he'd have to perform the chicken dance. The music started and...*Bawk!* The dancing began!

When he was finished grooving and clucking, Robin folded his arms. "Happy?" he sneered.

"You almost made me smile," said Raven. "Almost." She gave Robin a very serious look. "Now, don't say we didn't warn you. *Azarath Metrion Zinthos!*"

The spell was cast, and Robin was hit with magic. First he was changed from his birdlike self back to his normal one. And then he got...

Heat vision! He tried it out on Beast Boy, zapping heat blasts at his head and feet.

"Stop it!" cried Beast Boy.

Robin then tried out his new freeze breath. Unfortunately for Cyborg, Robin zeroed in on him!

"Come on!" complained Cyborg, frozen solid in a block of ice.

Super-speed was next, and he zoomed past Starfire. Then it was telekinesis time, which meant Robin could now move things with his mind. He concentrated hard and made a glass of water rise in the air—and spill on Raven's head!

"Really?" Raven said, understandably annoyed.

Robin jumped up and exclaimed, "This is awesome!"

"Just remember," began Raven. "With great power comes greater responsibility."

From inside his ice block, Cyborg added, "The burden you'll be asked to carry will be even bigger."

"You'll definitely be different from all of your friends, dude," Beast Boy told Robin.

Starfire, in her usual innocent way, added, "Did I mention we are having meatloaf for dinner?"

Raven turned back to Robin, her voice grave and serious. "Yes, Robin. You will be forever a stranger in a world that can never truly understand you."

"A curse…" said Beast Boy, in a spooky voice.

"A curse…" said Cyborg.

"A curse…" said Raven.

"Meatloaf…" said Starfire.

"Wrong!" replied Robin. "This is going to be GREAT!"

CHAPTER 5

Robin couldn't wait to try out his new superpowers and took off in search of a way to save Jump City from danger.

Raven shook her head. "Wait till he sees what it's really like."

Cyborg nodded. "He won't be smiling then."

"I almost feel sorry for the guy," said Beast Boy.

They didn't have to wait long to find out. Robin crashed through the window just a second later.

"I'm back!" he said.

Starfire blinked in confusion. "You were gone for less than a minute!" she said.

"Super-speed," answered Robin. "Thanks, Raven." He patted her on the head. She glared and growled at him.

"So you know the pain of having super-powers? The agony?" Cyborg asked Robin.

"Nope! It was great," Robin replied. "I rounded up every super-villain and put them in jail."

"In three seconds?" asked Beast Boy.

"I also used my powers to grow crops and solve world hunger," continued Robin. "I ended all wars, too." He looked smug.

"Oh, is that all?" Raven said sarcastically.

Robin zoomed over to the table. "Oh, and I made meatloaf for dinner."

"Joy!" gushed Starfire. But before she could enjoy any of the food, the bird Robin had used in his experiment came and took the meatloaf away.

Just then, Raven asked an important question. "So, you're saying you solved *all* the world's problems?"

"Uh-huh," Robin said proudly.

Starfire's eyes grew wide. "And there are no more super-villains to battle?" she asked.

"You know it!" said Robin.

Beast Boy sighed. "Then I guess we don't have to be Teen Titans anymore," he realized.

Robin nodded. "That's right—wait, WHAT??"

"Nice going, Robin," Cyborg said, annoyed. "You just put us all out of a job."

The Teen Titans then packed up their stuff.

"Guess this is good-bye," Beast Boy said, holding a box of his stuff under each arm.

79

Cyborg seemed to be fine with it. A simple "See ya," and he was out of there. Raven left with a quick "Later."

It was Starfire who was the most upset. "I will miss all of you," she said emotionally.

"Wait!" yelled Robin as the others left the Tower. "What am I going to do?"

Raven shrugged. "Get a new job, I guess."

CHAPTER 6

Inside the Corp-O office building, Robin was wearing a suit and tie, hoping to get a job. He nervously sat across a desk from a businessman, who looked over Robin's résumé.

"Let's see, it says here you worked for the Teen Titans," said the man.

"Yes, sir," Robin replied. "We were a team of super heroes."

"Were?" asked the man. "You were fired?"

Feeling a little uneasy, Robin pulled at his shirt collar. "Not fired. Just…disbanded. I kind of solved all the world's problems."

"Right," said the man. He looked down at the résumé again. "And under special skills, you listed X-ray vision?"

"Yup," Robin answered.

That's all the man needed to hear. He held out his hand to shake. "You start Monday."

Without any villains to fight, the weekend dragged for Robin. He was actually looking forward to starting his new job. When Monday came, he got to the office a little early and sat behind his desk. It only took a few minutes for it to feel quiet, lonely, and very, *very* boring.

So he passed the time by taking a nap,

warming up his coffee mug with his heat vision, and doodling. Man, was he bored! He looked at a framed picture of himself with the Teen Titans and let out a deep, sad sigh.

Twenty-five years later, Robin was middle-aged and riding a bus home from work. On his right, a mother was holding a crying baby, who spit up on Robin. On his left, a drooling old lady fell asleep on his shoulder. Robin used his telekinetic powers to push the lady off his shoulder, but a second later, she fell right back onto it.

When Robin arrived at his small, dingy apartment, he changed out of his uncomfortable suit. He used his heat vision to warm up some leftover pizza. Then it was a long night of bad TV to watch.

Forty-seven years after that, Robin was an old man. He sat in the park, feeding the birds...until that *same* bird he had used in his experiment stole his birdseed.

Back home, Robin struggled to walk. He

used his telekinetic powers to call his cane to him, but they were too weak, and the cane fell just short of his reach. Robin pitched forward—right on his face—and ended up going to the hospital.

As he lay in his hospital bed, hooked up to all sorts of machines and monitors, he shook his head sadly. "What happened?" he thought. "Where did it go wrong? Where did I lose my purpose?"

Just then, Robin had a realization. "Oh… it was when I got my superpowers." A single tear ran down his cheek. "They were right. These powers are a curse!"

Suddenly, the hospital curtain pulled back. There were the other Teen Titans (now pretty old themselves).

"In your face, Robin!" said Cyborg, now in a wheelchair.

"Vindication!" Beast Boy said as he held a walker.

Cyborg and Beast Boy did a little victory dance.

"Uh-huh! That's right!" sang Cyborg. "Super-powers are a curse, curse, curse, cursety, curse, curse, curse!"

Raven levitated over to Robin's bed. She now wore giant glasses to see better. She only had one thing to tell Robin:

"Told you so!"

BONUS ACTIVITY!

Uh-oh, Robin has had a little fender bender!

Can you spot the differences between these pictures of the Batmobile?

Here are some of the differences.

Can you spot more?